Curly Chrissy

Chrishuara Haynie

ISBN:

DEDICATION

This book is inspired by my beautiful great nieces Tete &
Nylah.

CONTENTS

ACKNOWLEDGMENTS

"I must start by thanking my awesome family. From reading early drafts to giving me advice on the cover, name, to providing a space for me to create. Thank you so much."
Family Always

1 MEET CURLY CHRISSY

There was a beautiful little black girl named Chrissy who was a very bright girl. Chrissy loved to play and eat delicious food. She was always happy to visit parks and gardens.

One morning, Chrissy had her breakfast and went out of her house. She found one of her friends with his parents and asked him, "Where are you going, my dear friend?"

The friend replied, "I am going to the park with my mom and dad."

As Chrissy heard so, she immediately got interested in going to the park with her mother.

She went to her mother and asked her to go to the park as soon as possible.

Then the mother said to the little girl, "Okay, we will go but not now. We will go there in the evening."

The little girl was a bit unhappy to hear that but did not immediately insist on going to the park.

Chrissy again went outside and found her best friend, John, sitting on a bench. She saw that he was eating some donuts. The donuts looked delicious. Chrissy loved to eat donuts, so she rushed to her mother and asked her, "Mother, can we go out and get some donuts? John is having some tasty donuts, and I want to eat some too."

The mother agreed to buy some donuts for Chrissy, but she asked her to wait until her household work is done.

Then suddenly, the mother brought an outfit and asked her daughter to wear it.

"What is it, mother?", questioned Chrissy to her mother.

To this, the mother replied, "Today is Juneteenth, and it is Juneteenth outfit, my sweetheart. You must wear it.

"What is Juneteenth, mother?" asked Chrissy to her mother.

"Juneteenth is a holiday in the United States to recall and show respect for the emancipation of the enslaved African Americans. It is celebrated on June nineteenth", answered the mother.

"But I do not like it, mother. It looks so boring. So, I am not going to wear it", uttered the little girl.

The mother got angry and said, "If you do not wear the Juneteenth outfit then neither will I take you to the park nor will I buy any donuts for you."

Chrissy got mad at her mother as Chrissy could not have or do the things she liked if she did not wear the Juneteenth outfit.

The upset little girl wanted to be alone, so she preferred to go to her favorite place, the tree house.

She climbed the tree and entered the treehouse like a mad guest. Then she began to cry.

Then suddenly, someone said, "Why are you crying?"

Listening to the strange voice, Chrissy looked everywhere and was surprised to find no human being around.

Then she noticed an owl saying, "It's me, Mr. Owl."

"Do not be surprised. I am a magical and intelligent owl who can talk. I am like a guardian to you. You can share everything with me", added the owl.

The little girl told the owl in a sad voice, "My mother wants me to wear a Juneteenth outfit today. But I do not want to do so. I think it is not necessary."

Listening to the little girl's words, Mr. Owl gave a smile and narrated the story of his brother. He said, "One day, a human caught my brother and put him in a cage. The human gave him good food, and clean water and took good care of him. The human never made him do any work."

"Then your brother must be pleased and satisfied with his life", asked the little girl to the owl.

"No. Not at all. As my brother was kept in the cage, he got very upset and depressed, " said Mr. Owl.

"So, when was he happy?" questioned Chrissy.

Then the owl replied, "When my brother came out of the cage and got his freedom, he was very much joyful."

"But can you think of the enslaved people? Their lives and their pain?" added the owl.

"Were they put in the cage?" asked the little girl.

"The house in which they were enslaved was no less than a cage. Moreover, unlike my brother, they were not given good food, water, or clothes to wear. In addition, they were mistreated and even beaten," said the owl to the little girl.

As Chrissy heard the words of Mr. Owl, she wanted to know more and more about the painful lives of the enslaved people in the old days.

"I want to know more about the slaves and the importance of Juneteenth," said the curious Chrissy to Mr. Owl.

Mr. Owl asked Chrissy to close her eyes. As the little girl closed her eyes, the magical owl flapped his wings. Chrissy felt like dreaming. With her closed eyes, she saw some circles. She tried her best to open her eyes, but she could not.

After some time, Chrissy opened her eyes and found herself in a strange land. She also found the owl sitting on her hand.

Chrissy found that she was standing near a port with many huge ships.

"Where are we?" asked Chrissy to the owl with astonishment.

"We are in Africa now. And we are not in 2022. We are in the 1800s. With magic, I have brought you here to show you something," uttered Mr. Owl.

2 JUNETEENTH

After some time, Chrissy opened her eyes and found herself in a strange land. She also found the owl sitting on her hand.

Chrissy found that she was standing near a port with many huge ships.

"Where are we?" asked Chrissy to the owl with astonishment.

"We are in Africa now. And we are not in 2022. We are in the 1800s. With magic, I have brought you here to show you something," uttered Mr. Owl.

"But don't you think it will be a blunder if anyone sees us and finds out that we are from the future?" the little girl asked the owl.

To this, the owl told the girl not to be worried about

it as no one would be able to see them because of his magic. The girl relaxed and stepped ahead to see what was happening on the huge ships.

The port looked quite crowded. Chrissy found many Africans getting on the ships. Their hands were tied with ropes. They were standing in a queue and boarding on the ship. Some white people were thrashing them with whips and were forcing them to move.

Chrissy got eager and asked the owl what was happening. To this, the owl replied, "The Africans are taken from their country and are forced to go to America and Europe. There they will be made slaves."

Then Chrissy saw a man, his wife, and a baby. They, too, were forced to leave Africa and be slaves.

The heartbreaking thing was that the man was sent to another ship, and the woman and her baby were made to board another ship.

In the next moment, Chrissy could see the woman cleaning and ironing the clothes, washing utensils, cooking, and taking care of the two kids of her master. She was mistreated in that house.

When her baby was crying, and she wanted to feed

him, the wife of the master said her, "Hey, you! Go and dress up my sons for an evening party". "But my son is crying, madam. Give me some time. I want to feed him."

Listening to this, the lady owner got angry and told her first to go and dress up her two sons, and then she would be allowed to feed her baby. So, the poor enslaved woman was forced to do so even though it was tough for her to hear her son crying.

Chrissy was watching everything. The little girl too, felt bad for the woman and her baby. She also felt that the enslaved woman was given a lot of work to do.

Suddenly, the owl flapped his wings again, and the little girl found herself in the kitchen. There she saw the enslaved woman cooking the food. Then she heard the lady owner say someone else to clean the dresses and iron them. Chrissy was happy as she thought the poor woman's work load was reduced. She told the owl, "Thank God! The workload on the woman is reduced. But who is doing the rest of the work?"

Mr. Owl replied, "It is Will, the son of the enslaved woman. He is ten years old and has to clean the dresses and iron them."

As Chrissy heard that she got too much unhappy.

She found the little boy had to clean a lot of clothes.

The next moment, the little girl found Will ironing the clean clothes. Then Chrissy noticed that the enslaved boy was looking out the window and watching the kids playing in the playground. Will, too wanted to go out and play with other kids, but he was not allowed to do so. Will just looked at the window and forgot that he was ironing the clothes. As a result, one of the clothes got burnt.

When the lady owner saw the burnt clothes, she got furious at Will and beat him. So, Will wept. The husband and wife decided to get rid of the little boy as soon as possible. It broke Chrissy's heart.

The next day, Chrissy heard the husband telling his wife, "I have talked with Mr. Grint, he wants to buy Will. We will sell him and finally, get rid of him."

Then the couple mentioned that to the enslaved woman and her son and asked Will to get ready to leave the house. As the poor woman and her son heard that, they started crying and asked their owners not to separate them.

Seeing this, Chrissy said to the owl, "This is just injustice. How can they do this to the poor woman and her little son?"

Mr. Owl did not speak anything, and he flapped his

wings again, and the little girl found herself in a cotton mill. There she discovered Will working hard.

"So sad of Will. He has to do hard things at such a young age. I feel sorry for him," said the little girl to the owl.

She even found Will eating stale corn meal, lard, and some peas.

Then she found him going to his new owner and saying, " Master, my dress is torn. Can you please get some clothes for me? My mother used to stitch them for me but now I am not able to do so."

"Get off. I can not get any clothes for you," the owner angrily said.

"But this is injustice", uttered the little boy.

Hearing Will's words, the owner got even angrier. He said, " I have heard you are very good at cleaning clothes. So, go to the washroom and clean my clothes."

Seeing all this, Chrissy got annoyed with the new owner. She saw that the next morning, Will was very happy. She asked the reason behind his happiness to the owl.

The owl said, "Today is June nineteenth, the

Juneteenth day. The federal troops have taken control of the state and have ensured that all the enslaved people are set free. So, it means Will and his mother are too free", said the owl.

Soon, Chrissy found Will and his mother hugging each other. They were very happy.

Then all of a sudden, Chrissy opened her eyes. She found herself back in the tree house. She saw that Mr. Owl smiled and flew up in the sky. She stepped down from the tree.

Then suddenly, she found the tree talking to her. This time, she was not surprised to see the magical talking tree.

The tree told her, "Today, you must have learned the importance of Juneteenth. You must have felt the pain of the enslaved people. You get so many delicious things to eat, but they had just stale food. You have good clothes to wear, but they didn't. You are free to play in the playground, but they were not."

"You must apologize before your mother and then teach the importance of Juneteenth to your friends", added the talking tree.

"Yes, definitely", said Chrissy.

Soon she ran to her mother and apologized for her

bad behavior. She immediately wore the Juneteenth outfit and rushed outside to show it to her friends.

One of her friends asked her why she was wearing the Juneteenth outfit. To this, Chrissy explained everything she learned and taught him why it was necessary to celebrate Juneteenth.

As Chrissy's mother saw that she got very much glad. Soon, she took her to the park and bought some donuts for her. That day, Chrissy and her friends learned about Juneteenth and celebrated it every year with pleasure.

Coloring Activity

Juneteenth

Juneteenth Celebration

```
H P C N Y N L C J E U Q E E W K F T C K O L A B
N O I T A M A L C O R P A V R Q M R U H A E U W
W A R B E S R W C O M M U N I T Y W H U F K G L
G E G A W S O U T H Q R U B L M Y W F Y G D Z K
X R C C W O R P Q J I I I H B A T P E J N T C A
G P L O B S O F D W R W T Y V B V Z B J Q D B F
V D T E H V Z G H N V J A K S I Z Y P X P P G R
E P G P U J U G U G W I D M B M N A Y C W A O I
Z E I N S P C Q Q R T L C O N F E D E R A T E C
S B N E U E K X K K J U N E T E E N T H B Z N A
H T S W R X F G V D X M Y M V F J A V G T T G N
O H A S R U O Q A Z V I U L K X J T U X P Q C A
L P Q Y E P H S S R W W O M F P V E O G V F B M
I E M S N U F Y R E V A L S Y H S T G E Z O U E
D M D M D J E Q P S M O V E M E N T X T Q M I R
A S M D E E H M Q Q M A W M B I N V B Y V M F I
Y J Q V R U K S K B L C R X C S X G I K T W Z C
X E A N L O C N I L M A H A R B A R S Y Y C P A
R N W F Y L T C L J P L G S O E C B P X M W R N
B C I D P O Z H R V W A K J F R E L H G N A S V
Q Z Q R Y N V G E E M A N C I P A T I O N R G D
Y J O L L A N O I T A N C B B F N X I L N F S X
G B W U Z X S Y A S I S J I D N A G C R C A U F
T M B R E W O I V N B E A S C L D C W O R Z W Y
```

Abraham Lincoln	African American	Community	Confederate
Emancipation	Holiday	Juneteenth	Movement
National	News	Proclamation	Slavery
South	Surrender		

ABOUT THE AUTHOR

Chrishuara Haynie was born in 1983 in Dallas, Texas. Growing up, she was fascinated with writing, acting, the creative arts. This interest led to some early exposure to creating plays, modeling, acting. Mrs. Haynie, who now acts, a publicist, author has developed a passion for many ideas, and Curly Chrissy is one. Chrishuara explores the issue of how children, especially in the African American community do not know events, history, and or facts of their culture. By Curly Chrissy she gives the kids the ability to learn about past events, while educating them on current issues and delivering a message for the future. Curly Chrissy is Mrs. Haynie's first children book.

www.ingramcontent.com/pod-product-compliance
Lightning Source LLC
Chambersburg PA
CBHW020121180726
47992CB00019B/1427